The Best Toy

by Sarah Nash

illustrated by Pamela Venus

Tamarind Ltd

"What toy would you like, Sam?"

"The best one, Dad!"

"Would you like this one?"

"Too fast."

Puttt...
Puttt...
Puttt...

"Too jumpy, Dad."

"Too messy."

Look... look....

"We'll never find the best toy."

Hello..

Choose me.

"Found it. This is the BEST toy."